The Red Khémèresh

Mab Morris

With a foreword by
Rosemary Lévy Zumwalt

Dedicated to Ida G. Boers
For all the years of supporting me, and believing in me!

Thank you, Claire Ryan, for helping make this project happen. So many thanks to Kathryn Hinds for years of discussing writing, and deep friendship. So many experiences in the writing and editing field came largely thanks to you. My deep gratitude to Rosemary Lévy Zumwalt, not only in profound experiences of caring for your mother, but helping me know that my own research with the inspiration for the story had indeed crafted something special.

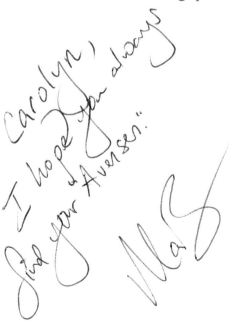

Contents

Foreword

As an anthropologist and folklorist, I am an enthusiastic reader of Mab Morris's The Red Khémèresh. I have done research on the shamanistic rituals of the native peoples of the circumpolar region. Specifically I have done fieldwork in Point Hope, Alaska, on the Nalukataq ceremony, which is held to honor and celebrate the spirit of the bowhead whale. I have written about this in "The Return of the Whale: Nalukataq, the Point Hope Whale Festival." Additionally I have researched and written on Sedna, the powerful deity of the sea, in "The Sea Spirit of the Central Eskimo and her Relationship to the Living: A Delicate Balance." I give these professional details to provide context for my remarks on Mab Morris's work.

Artfully fluent in the literature of Siberian

7

shamanism, Morris has taken the ethnographic details and has woven a fantasy world of power and beauty. Her Bogeh [shaman] uses the power of word, of sound, of music, of sight and of the un-seen as seen through the eyes of those who can see. This shaman has the power of her gender, for Mab has thankfully created Phayaden as the female Bogeh.

In my research on shamanistic rituals of the native peoples of the circumpolar region, I have noted the de-emphasis on female shaman in the ethnographic literature. But these powerful women shamans were and are present. One simply has to read past the unfortunate male-centric bias in the writings of anthropologists.

Mab Morris's writing is both sparse and magical in keeping with the sweep of the steppes. She has created a world of the Tashihyel. The reader is centered with the Bhaganev, the world tree, and is gripped by the power of the Bogeh.

As a reader of fantasy fiction myself, I relish seeing The Red Khémèresh in print. As an anthropology professor, I see an opportunity for a creative use for this work in the classroom, paired with readings on Siberian shamanism. This reader is left wanting to read more – one hopes that a sequel to The Red Khémèresh is in the making.

Rosemary Lévy Zumwalt

Professor Émerita of Anthropology

Agnes Scott College

Decatur, Georgia

Mab Morris

I

The shreds of the book lay in Phayaden's arms. Each page she had found had been torn by the wind, trampled by a herd of horses into the rocky frozen ground. They seemed like wounded soldiers on the battlefield, or the bodies of the dead. She'd almost walked past them; it was such a useless book. But she knew words had power. Passing one forlorn page, she'd turned back, *Bogeh* enough—shaman enough—still, to sense the rising echoes of its words.

With her horse following, often breathing warm air on her shoulder or lipping her braids, Phayaden picked up each page she could find. She did not know how the book had come to be lost and torn in the Tashihyel, land of felt tents and horse riders. Perhaps it did not matter how this book of rare rice paper had become strewn across the landscape, of words that only a few in her land could read.

She already owned a precious copy of *The Khémèresh* by Teyeb and Ushar that discussed things unknown in the *ihyel*, of the *vhagas* and other mysteries written for *Bogeh* like her, or those they called shaman to the north. She feared that many *Bogeh* did not realize that the *ihyel* was not just the land, and meant more than their country, the Tashihyel, but encompassed the entire mysterious reaches beyond the borders of their land. It went far beyond even the countries beyond the steppes of the Tashihyel, even as it was also just the earth beneath her feet. *Vhagas* was a sound that meant more than that which echoed unseen on the other side of the trees, or was found through the smoke hole of any felt gher. Few of the younger shamans seemed to understand the full meanings rising from the *Khémèresh* terms. Phayaden hesitated to call them *Bogeh*. They could barely read *The Khémèresh*, that holiest of books, or denied its mystery. Somehow Phayaden knew that this book—this torn one in her arms—was the only real copy. What rose from the book was an easy vision to carry, and she was grateful it was not more: Without ever reading a written word from any of the tattered pages, she knew that this copy said what none of the other copies read by any other *Bogeh* in the Tashihyel could tell. The land was broken, just as this Book was broken.

How long it had been broken, she did not know; she'd seen echoes of it in the visions that had driven her from her studies as a *Bogeh*. She knew it better now with this book in her hands. Small clans and families led by a chief, uniting or fighting with other clans and families, fighting for pasturage, fighting against the peoples to the north, to the east and south, but rarely to the west. Demons lived in the western mountains. Everyone in the Tashihyel lived with this brokenness, but did not see it.

She could not put the book in the horse's

saddlebags. The thought was unbearable. Clenched to her chest as it was, she could not even let it go enough to grab her saddle horn, pull herself up, to sit astride her horse. She walked with the broken book protected in her arms. Following the hoof prints of the goats, camels and horses… mainly horses, Phayaden walked over a hill in this seemingly flat land, an ocean of emptiness.

Clutching the broken book, the veil of *vhagas* from the book's secret echo was rent yet again.

She had not untied her braids and let them fall over her eyes, to be a veil between the more material *ihyel* and the unseen *vhagas*. She was not in a felt gher, chanting, and letting her vision rise up the supporting beam, the false tree, rising up through the smoke hole and into *vhagas*. She was in the *ihyel*. Standing on the ground of the vast steppes of the Tashihyel. And yet: There He stood.

He. A Rider. His body sleek and strong, his back to her. The Horse stomped His left fore hoof not in anger, but with the sheer energy he contained in the placid space where they both calmly waited. They'd waited centuries, or just this one moment. Rider and Horse. The rider rode bare backed, without reins. The muscles of both were strong and lithe. They nearly filled the sky. Both a dusty red. She did not see much of The Rider's face, but He turned His head to acknowledge her.

And then... Over His shoulder came, briefly, something like light and brilliant with Words.

The moment was then gone. The Rider, seeing that she had seen, nodded and moved on. Within the *u'wuhshu* silence that came in their wake there was also the echoes of hoof beats came the sounds of clashing swords, shot bows, and desperate cries. War, unlike the land had ever seen—beyond invasion and clan fights—was coming. She trembled. The land would need a leader.

Phayaden stood on the ground, in the *ihyel*, and

waited till the sounds in the *vhagas* faded. She thought for a moment, standing still in the silence and daylight, knowing that her family's ghers were beyond one rise. Her mare rested her muzzle on Phayaden's shoulder, huffing into her ear. Phayaden looked up at her, patted her on her nose, and finally put the broken book into her saddlebags and lifted herself astride her horse. The last vision had been too much; riding was far simpler. Visions like that had been why she'd run away from her duties two years before, and returned to her family.

She stopped the horse once, as they looked down at the lake where her mother must be washing clothes with her aunt, and at the two round felt ghers her family lived in, and the herd of horses nearby. The *u'wuhshu* had taken her, that silent, lingering peace rising from magical nature. Phayaden did not want to speak, but knew she must, or she would carry its silence with her into the gher. Even if no one else noticed, it would jangle with all the other noises and words of the world, and it would pain her. She had returned to her family because of visions too large for her to carry, so that she could be herself and love her family and a simple life. And here again, she was not merely a daughter or niece, she was a *Bogeh* carrying a broken book and all the mysteries that came with it.

Swallowing, she spoke to the horse.

"It was not the book, or the vision that was strange, was it?" she asked. "Even for you? I do not know if you feel the *u'wuhshu* power which came with the book and the vision, and made their echo clear." She smiled. "I think you were worried most about not being ridden. Strangest thing of all."

The mare snorted, nodding her head. Phayaden smiled.

"Even if I am a mad *Bogeh*?"

The horse, as well as her family, could expect a *Bogeh* to have visions, but that any man, woman or child of the Tashihyel would rather walk than ride? Never!

They started forward. She could be silent now, not speaking of her trip. Her silence would not carry the *u'wuhshu* with it, the unworldly stillness she did not want to share. She had not become a *Bogeh* because her family had little sense of the *vhagas* beyond the material world. They had a sense of the *vhagas*, but not enough to become *Bogeh*. And Phayaden was not supposed to have visions or sense things any longer, for she was mad. Insane.

Stopping at her felt tent, she removed first the book, and then the herbs she had found, and roots. She did at least this, the gathering of herbs, hoping she could find ones for healing, for her knowledge of healing plants was much greater than any others of her family. She must contribute something from her studies if she denied them her vision, as she had not undone her braids to claim that she was a normal woman. Phayaden knew she was not, still. And she must not be idle. As she stepped over the threshold, she touched the doorjamb in thanks to the spirits, and then reached out to the table by the *bhaganhev* rising up the center which she did not touch. She looked up at its carvings and slowly let her eyes travel up this false tree to the smoke hole in the center. With a deep breath, she laid the herbs on the table, and then took the book to where her rolled up pallet lay, found a woven bag, took everything out of it, and put the broken book inside.

The bag she hid as best she could, and then went back outside to tend her patient horse.

"She is good to you, today?" asked her brother, Paybas, who was already working with the saddle.

"Yes." Phayaden helped him take off the saddle and bridle, which they lay inside the gher.

"Did you find anything of use to you?" he asked.

Phayaden looked up at him. His words and his face had a false lightness. She could see the deception in the tightness around his eyes, however. Her family knew something had gone wrong with her, but did not know what.

"Some *toub* and *falleh*," she said holding out one of the root vegetables, and the herbs for him to see. "But that is all."

He nodded then shrugged. "It is for our meal tonight?"

"Enough *toub* for many nights," she said, leaning close to him, as they led the horse back to the picket, "or for some *walika*?" Their uncle Dhuma was renowned for making good use of the root to make the powerful spirituous drink.

"Oh aye?" he said with a grin. "We must give that to uncle, then."

She nodded. "I left most of it in the saddle bag. You will take care of it?"

"Indeed. But look, what is this on the hill?"

She had to look over his shoulder, and past the embroidery of his sleeve as Paybas pointed. There were riders in the distance headed towards them, still too far to read any banners.

With one look she undid the tie on her braids and shook them out, but ever careful to keep them from her eyes. "We must saddle her up again," she said, and nodded to where their uncle Dhuma was also sliding onto his saddle.

As they saddled her horse, Dhuma said to her brother, "Ware the dogs; these strangers will think it strange till they see your sister, that we ride up to meet them."

She climbed onto her saddle, and they rode to meet the newcomers.

"Well Phaya," Uncle Dhuma said to her, "with hope your braids are still good for something. What enemy would attack a *Bogeh*'s family?" He paused. "What if they come to find you, and need your vision?"

Phayaden hoped they would not need her to stand, or even dance, near a gher's supporting post to enter into a trance and see into the other world.

She shrugged. "We shall see, first, what it is they want. I can always guide with logic, even if I will not climb the *bhaganhev* and rise into the *vhagas*. Logic is as good a guide as the spirit. But perhaps they will wish for the *toub* I found, which is sad. Paybas and I hoped you would have good use for it."

"Eh? Oh well, perhaps the *toub* will sweeten their visit for this day." Dhuma was jovial. The trimmed hairs of his mustache and beard only emphasized his smile, echoing the fan of laugh lines around his eyes. "Besides, *walika* can fool men's minds if they drink too much, even as it delights us all."

The riders held no banners, and yet the company was large. One man, riding in the lead, left the group and galloped towards them.

"Dhuma! Phaya!" he cried.

"It is Tengis!" Dhuma said and raced forward with a shout of joy and welcome.

Phayaden smiled and followed more slowly, for

22

the decorum required of both a *Bogeh* and a woman. Tengis was a friend of their small clan. He was not one who would fight them over pasturage, and he was also a dear friend to her—and had been the one to bring her back to her family, when her visions had become too much.

Dhuma and Tengis embraced like wrestlers, still standing in their stirrups. They were near in height, Phayaden observed, though it was clear that one had more wealth than the other. They both had long dark hair tied back under their hats. Tengis was the larger man, with strength you could see through his clothes, somehow echoed in the lines of embroidery and leather. Dhuma was getting a bit thick around the middle. Still standing, Tengis rose up straighter, and clapped the older man on the back heartily and looked to Phayaden with warmth. Phayaden could not embrace him like a man, but she smiled her joy.

"You ware yourselves with your *Bogeh*, I see,"

said Tengis. "Wise precaution, as you are a small family traveling alone."

"Come, Phayaden found much *toub*, and we will all feast tonight, if you will stay with us?"

"That was my hope."

"I will go and tell my wife and sister."

"And I would speak to Phaya," Tengis said.

Dhuma rode back to the ghers, where the family waited for knowledge. From this distance Phayaden could see her family milling about nervously. They did not reveal their weapons, but they were a small family and it would have been disastrous for them to fight. Her mother's hands were clasped together, over her heart. Her aunt was gesturing to the few girls still outside to get into the gher. They would be in reach of their bows this way, but also unseen by strange men.

Phayaden wondered if Tengis needed her counsel again. He had often come to the *Bogeh* School for counsel of her elders, but found himself leaning on her words more often. They had both struggled with visions that seemed too large for their status, though their visions were of a different sort. With the book in a bag in her gher, she now knew he'd seen the broken Tashihyel as well, and she realized, now, that what little she'd been able to express of her old visions had been woven into her prior counsel.

"So how are you?" she asked Tengis.

"Well, though I have not seen any that I might call family in a long time."

"Not even your brother Jekente?"

"He has wandered off with a clan of his own, and resents that I have become chief of the Rheshi."

She smiled, "He would wish to be chief, I think."

"But he has no vision," Tengis said. "No vision for what his people could be, or how to lead them there."

"As you always have," Phayaden said. She wondered how he could pursue something so great and still forget that this meant he must be great as well. She guessed that he had already experienced some tests to his convictions, his vision. Her *Bogeh* sight said his tests were unfinished, however.

"Was that a foolish thing, you think? A foolish hope, my vision for our people?"

She shook her head, "How could I think it foolish, Tengis? And me a *Bogeh*? We deal with vision to guide men's lives, or should. I would have to be more mad than I thought, and…." She stopped for something with these words rang out in her mind. She could see the footfall of a Horse that filled the skies, and hear one tiny echo within it—not the sound of it, or what it was, only that it was there. Another hint at war.

"You look very *Bogeh*, just now," he said.

She shook her head, but smiled at him. "I have been finding things in the Tashihyel." She realized she was about to speak of The Red Rider, but could not. He knew she had run from visions very much like this. She shifted her thoughts to the oddity she'd brought to her family three days earlier. "I found a man. Alone! With only a horse and an eagle."

Tengis was suitably surprised. "No gher?"

She shook her head. "A hair-house for one man? He has no braids, but I think he is more *Bogeh* than my master. He plays a flute, and he knows how to play my *ushadaz*."

"And that does not bother you?" His words were soft, but the lines around his eyes tightened with concern.

"The way he plays does not… send me into the unseen. And the family is glad to hear good music again."

He lifted a hand and reached over and gently touched away the tear.

"It had been too much," she said, "But truly, he plays well. I am happy you will hear him."

"Then I am at peace."

"Music is not always a *Bogeh* thing, and I keep

my braids from my eyes." She smiled at him. "Thank you for finding me and bringing me home. Jekente did not understand."

"No, my brother couldn't. And even I only knew you'd been unhappy… and had wandered.

She said nothing. She had not been able to explain then, but Tengis understood vision, even though his were not the same as hers. There were few places in the Tashihyel of permanence. There were meeting places like Gheber Rocks, and times when clan chiefs tried to meet in peace. There was one place of study for Bogeh. A stone building surrounded by felt ghers and garden of healing herbs. People came for healing, and chiefs would go there for advice if they did not already have a Bogeh travelling with them. Sometimes young men, searching for glory, would come for visions. Jekente had been one of them. He'd lingered as a friend, being Tengis' blood brother, claiming he wanted to strengthen clan affiliations. He'd implied much, but never declared anything. He'd been there when her visions began to be too large, and came upon a whim. He'd left. What little root to the *ihyel* he'd given her was gone. And one day, when she became lost in the vhagas, she'd wandered into the steppes, and gotten lost. Had she not known the land she'd have starved. Tengis somehow heard of it, had tracked her, and by her request brought her to her family.

Defying custom, Tengis took the reins of her horse, and slowed both their horses to stand. He took her hand. "Phaya, you must understand. Jekente could not help. Even your teachers could not. You must accept that."

After a moment she nodded. "I did not expect him to. I had wanted a friend. It is not from that I wanted to hide away from."

"I know this too. Even then you could not explain what you see. Even your teachers could not help you. But to just abandon you, that he did not help you…"

She sighed. "We had been such good friends. I thought we were, but he..." she could not finish the thought. She shook her head. "Perhaps there was too much confusion between us, and I was too strange a thing."

"Not so strange you could not give me good counsel, even then!"

"You were a good friend, Tengis." She was glad of the warmth of friendship the mere touch of his hand gave to her.

"Enough, now, Phaya," he said gently. He squeezed her hand. "You hurt too long on this, and now my men are come, and we are here. Your family awaits us."

She nodded, rallied, and helped Tengis and his men set their ghers. This done, they all crowded into Dhuma's gher and feasted. There were enough people in the gher that had there not been cloth over the movable walls the circular hut, no one would be able to see the lattice walls. The room was bright with embroidered satin of many colors, and smelled rich with festive foods, some of which Phayaden knew was being kept warm in her own gher. Phayaden brought out a man from the crowd to the center. He held her *ushadaz.* He was tall, thin and wiry, almost as if he were another *bhaganhev* supporting the center of the gher. He had no beard or hair on his head. His clothes looked worn by wind and time, decorated only by metal rings to tie one side and overlap another to protect him against the elements. He face was like his coat with the cracked look of wet and then dried leather, and curiously stained by more than rain.

"This is Engidu. He will play for us," she said.

Engidu said nothing, merely bowed at Dhuma and Tengis. "Well met, Tengis," Engidu said, and smiled.

Phayaden felt a flash of the *u'wuhshu* power as he spoke. But it was gone so quickly, she thought it must

31

just have been that his blue eyes suddenly seemed brighter within his weathered face, a chance gleam of the brazier's fire. He sat down and began pulling the bow across the *ushadaz's* three strings. Phayaden chimed the bells as he sang.

Engidu sang songs of horses, of the Tashihyel, with the wind, the sudden storms, the cold ground, a land riddled with rocks and holes of ground rats. He sang songs that echoed the imagery of the Tashihyel being an ocean, with the sound of the *ushadaz* making not just the sound of a horse ride, but also the sound of wind upon the summer grasses, of its silence, of its great vastness, and emptiness.

"I see what you mean," whispered Tengis to Phayaden when Engidu stopped to drink some plain water. "His playing travels this wide land, but without rising past the trees, or the *bhaganhev*, so we can all see it," he said, pointing to the carved post at the tent's center. "He is an odd one, is he not?"

"Yes, perhaps that is why I like him."

Phayaden smiled at him, leaning as close as was proper. This close she could see the vibrant colors of the embroidered felt, silk and the leather of his clothes. She could smell the rich sweat of him mingled with the smell of horse. It reminded her of the spices she'd brought her mother when she'd returned from the school, carefully horded for festival foods.

Tengis was suddenly alert. She could feel his body stiffen, and then he turned to the door just as the dogs of both camps began to bark. His men and her family erupted, rushing to the wall where the weapons were kept. Engidu came to her, thrusting the *ushadaz* into her arms.

"You... do not move from here," he said, and merged with the boiling mass of people that streamed into the night.

The younger children crowded around her aunt and mother; they looked like a colorful jumble of clothes dotted with frightened faces. Phayaden looked at the *ushadaz* in her hands. It was not just a musician's instrument. It was a *Bogeh* instrument. Suddenly looking at the box, and the hole, and the strings laying across it... she trembled for the book she'd hidden that day. This *ushadaz* was nothing. If she had one treasured object as a shaman it was the torn sheets of paper in a worn bag by her bed.

She dropped the instrument. The wood rang hollow on the ground and the strings wailed softly, then died as Phayaden crossed the threshold of her uncle's gher to go to her own.

She did not mind the sounds of the fighting. She could hear the hooves of the Horse she'd seen earlier ringing in her mind. Feeling as if she ran beneath the shadow of one mighty, red hoof, Phayaden ran to the other gher, stepped through the doorway, and into the shadows of the gher and shut the door.

With one step she knew she was not alone.

34

"Who…" she asked, afraid. She knew that it was not a friend.

He said nothing. He moved, a shadow, into the low glow from the brazier where her mother had left some food to warm. There was silence. She could not even hear the fighting through the lattice and felt walls. This was strange. More strange and fearsome than seeing a Rider filling the sky.

"What? How?" she asked. She started to turn, to run out the door.

He grabbed her, pulled her back, and slammed her against the gher's center *bhaganhev*, knocking the brazier, coals, and pot of stew.

Mab Morris

II

One hand around her throat, the other with a knife poised to strike.

Jekente's face was tight and red. His eyes flashed in the firelight. He moved his hand from Phayaden's throat, to her mouth. She gasped for breath through her nose.

"Not one word," he said as he shifted his grip on his knife, to a back handed grip. Something strange looked out of his eyes filling the gher with *u'wuhshu* silence, but it was suddenly gathered up into the eyes of the young man she knew.

She tried to shake her head, to see the thing inside Jekente again, to fight, also, to escape. She could not breathe or speak. Could not understand why he was there at that moment. Fighting her family. Fighting his brother. Fighting her.

His eyes grew bright as he shifted his grip to cover more of her nose.

He was angry with her, and she could not see why.

"You are with my brother."

She had known that there was some confusion between them, but she had been *Bogeh*, and he had gone his path. He had left without a promise *to* her, or asking for any *from* her. She had never imagined there was a question of choice, or loyalty between them, or his blood brother. She had felt guilty, but glad he had left. There had always been a ringing in her mind of something she had missed, a word, or an expression. Here it was full flower, gone wrong. She tried to pull his arm down, push him, kick him, fight him as she tried to breathe.

He cut her hands or arms, casually, with his knife each time she came close to hurting him. She flailed, and struggled. He calmly cut her. She scratched his cheek, and he sliced her hand. She tried to knee him, and he sliced her shoulder. He was now calm, as if he had time.

She was not a weak woman, but he was strong. He had the threat of knife, physical force, and sheer surprise.

Slowly the sounds of violence and war returned around her gher. When it was loud, as if close outside, he threw her to the rugs, into the scattered coals, still hot amid the spilled stew.

She gasped. "I didn't…" she began, unable to do more than croak. "We didn't…" she tried to reason with him.

He punched her with the butt of his knife. The blade sliced into her cheek, not deep. She recoiled.

He slammed the blade down, capturing her head wrap and braids, as he embedded the blade into the rug and dirt beneath it.

Her whole body shook as she realized how close he had come to slicing her ear, and how much strength he'd used. Another knife; he cut open her shirt. As she tried to stop him, he hit her head into the knife embedded into the ground. It cut into her ear and scalp.

His eyes burned with that strange gleam. She stared into them. A few seconds seemed to last a lifetime of silence, strangely akin to the deepening of the *u'wuhshu*. She felt herself rise into the dark, drawn into those eyes. She floated into the *vhagas* and stared into the eyes of something decidedly *not* Tengis's brother. It was darker, stranger, more twisted than the Red Rider that rode to war. Her blood pounded and she heard hoof beats, like drums and the clang of swords to war.

She felt Jekente's hands warm around her breast and along her waist. She gasped, plunged back into her body. "Jekente, please no," she said, confused, still sensing an echo of *vhagas*, redness, and the Horsemen.

He punched her. Again the blade cut her ear.

Her mind woke with blood and pain. All her senses came crashing into focus, surging with a roar.

Fury hit her, and she punched at him, crunching her stomach into her blow, ignoring the cutting blade by her head.

He grabbed her arms, pushed them over her head, slamming his free blade into the ground, catching her sleeves near her wrists, binding them to the ground.

His hands went to her pants, wrapped around the silk waistband, ready to tear it apart by sheer force.

The door burst open. Engidu boiled into the room. "Humna!" Engidu roared.

Tengis followed. Both men's faces and bodies seemed hot with anger. Phayaden felt the wave of it wash over her.

Jekente's face turned into a grimace of triumph. Phayaden realized he'd wanted them to come more than he'd wanted the attack on Phayaden. With a sound like glee that she heard only in the *vhagas*, Jekente turned and launched himself at Engidu, pulling both blades out of the ground, slicing again into Phayaden's arms and head.

Phayaden curled herself into a ball. Biting down on her pain, she took a deep breath. She watched Tengis attempt to strike his brother, knocking Engidu out of his way. Jekente slashed with both knives, but Tengis blocked him with his own blades. Jekente roared something incoherent at Engidu and launched himself, blades cutting through the wall of the gher with a sound of splintering wood and tearing fabric.

Both men followed, and Phayaden listened as the sounds of battle faded.

What serious breach had happened between the two blood brothers? Phayaden had never heard of brothers fighting like this before. The attack on her? Bewildering. It was as strange and terrible and awful as some of the more difficult visions she'd had from the *vhagas*. She curled up. It was a difficult vision from the *vhagas*, yet without the reassuring sense of the *u'wuhshu*, but tinged with the same red of the

Horseman. This vision walked in the world, in the *ihyel,* in the body of Tengis' brother.

She knew that she ought to look to her wounds, stop them from bleeding, but she could not move. She shivered in the cold from the open door, the broken gher, and a chill deep inside.

Engidu returned, bringing water and bandages. "We need to make sure that we stop the bleeding or you will hurt more, and be too weak to ride. We must ride. He will come back."

"He has left," she said, and knew it. "He did not win. Why come back?"

"He must come back; he must attempt to defeat his brother."

"Jekente was not fighting his brother."

Engidu sat back, eyebrows knit together with painful thoughts. "Yes. You are correct. I do not know why he first had business with you." He then looked at her, with eyes older than the Tashihyel. "Would you like him to come back and finish, or would you prefer to find the strength to defeat him?"

"Defeat him," she said as he bound the cut on her wrist, which was no longer bleeding as freely. The blade had missed the veins on one wrist, but had come close to the other.

"One cut on your ear is deep, though most of the cuts on your head are not deep. I have bound your wrist as well, though that was a near thing. You cannot afford to bleed more. We will ride soon."

He growled when she nodded and said, "Thank you. Tell me of the damage outside? What have we lost?"

Engidu told her while he cleaned her up and bandaged her wounds. He cauterized the dangerous one on her wrist, as it continued to bleed despite his binding. He refused to do the same with the one on her ear and head. "You cannot lose your looks yet."

"And what would you do?" she said, impatient,

wanting to get on with assessing the damage herself.

He took out the finest needle and some thread from his coat, and told her to hold still. "If I do this, your hair will grow back, and your ear will not flap."

"Perhaps we can put an earring in there?" she said flippantly.

He laughed and said, "Perhaps." It was not till later that she realized he had taken a metal ring from his clothes and sewn the cut around it. It was a fine thing, almost fit for decoration, holding a bead of pearl or some such stone.

Tengis came in through the door, stepping over the threshold. "I am going," he said.

"You agreed to wait for Phayaden and Dhuma's family," Engidu said

"They will be too slow."

Phayaden gasped when Engidu moved, moving faster than any man she'd ever seen. He blocked the door and the opening. "You told me you would help

Phayaden. You agreed, Tengis."

"I changed my mind. They will slow me down and I will not be able to catch up to Jekente in time."

"He will come and find you. You do not need to worry about finding him."

Tengis stiffened. "If I do not fight him on ground of my own choosing then I will not defeat him. You would prevent me from leaving?"

"I would prevent you from breaking your word."

"Going after my brother I will help her."

"No, you will not. You will see. He is gone. Your man will come back soon and tell you he could not find the tracks."

Phayaden knew it was with a very *Bogeh* authority that Engidu spoke. She was tired and wanted to cry, for more of the *vhagas* was in the gher than it ever had been. She did not know how much of it Tengis sensed, if he realized that this strange man spoke his prediction as a *Bogeh*.

46

"You know this?" Tengis asked.

"Yes. I know this." And Phayaden knew it too, and curled up in a ball again.

"You know nothing, musician," Tengis said and started towards the door.

Engidu did not move.

"Move," Tengis ordered.

"No."

Tengis threw a punch. Engidu blocked him, and used the block to throw Tengis back into the room.

Tengis flew over the stove to a carved chest on the other side of the room, crashing into furniture. He lifted himself and came around, but Engidu threw him again. The next time Tengis approached, they grappled. Engidu was faster and somehow stronger, skinny as he was. When he was done throwing him about the room, he wrestled Tengis, and quickly had him down. Then, Engidu sat on top of the chief of the Rheshi people, and son of the great Toberackhs.

Though Tengis struggled to get up, throw Engidu, or shift him, the man was as immovable as a mountain. Engidu did not even struggle to keep him down. Phayaden sat up. Even this was very *Bogeh*. Just this sitting. Being immovable.

"Why do men always think I cannot fight?" Engidu asked Phayaden.

"How would I know? I wish that I could have placed bets." Though she would, of course, have lost, since she would have bet on Tengis. "You do not look like you could lift a flute much less throw a man that distance with one arm."

He shrugged, "Now Tengis, will you listen to reason now, or the fact that I will keep you on your path by force if necessary?"

"Ow! My ribs! I think you broke a rib."

"You'll live, and be strong enough to fight the man who is your brother, Jekente. So, will you wait for Dhuma and his people?"

"Yes."

"You will not regret it."

Tengis said nothing.

"Tengis," Phayaden said, "perhaps you should talk to Dhuma about my family travelling with you."

Tengis was silent for a moment. She could see that he was angry, and ashamed. His brother had attacked him, and not just him, but a *Bogeh*, had almost raped her. "It is a thought. But. I will stay with you."

"You will need, at least, the care of women, and even me, for healing," she said, "if your brother is to attack again. Is it not your father who said one must always listen to the wisdom of one's women?"

"You are not my woman."

For some reason the words rang inside the damaged gher. Despite the colorful reds and greens, only slightly faded with time, they seemed to bounce off the broken wood, the burnt wool carpets, and then seemed to hang like smoke in the air. Whatever he said, they were bound together, and the words hurt her.

"Fine. I yield!" said Tengis. "Will you rise?"

Engidu stood up. "Do not doubt I will fight you again if you cross me, or break your word."

"I did not swear to you that I would not leave Phayaden and her family."

"You said you would not. If you say such a thing to me, then it is as good as a promise. A vow. Do not mistake me again." Phayaden wondered how stubborn a man Tengis must be, to defy Engidu's *Bogeh*-like authority.

"You believe this?"

"What is your word if you falter again? Do you wish to challenge it again? A man who would put loyalty above all else?"

Then Phayaden saw something she knew would make Tengis a great leader: the ability to trust the knowledge of great men. Tengis lifted his hands and smiled. "My word would be nothing, Engidu. Would that

I could have bet against myself. For all my bruises and broken bones, I would have been rich."

Engidu laughed. "Greet your scout. Here he comes now. Go and see."

Tengis left the gher, but stood by the open door. The scout came into the light of the outdoor fire. He shook his head. "I do not understand, my chief, but his trail, and that of his men disappeared, faded…as if swept by the wind."

Tengis looked at Engidu, inside the gher, then back at his man. "Not even one trail your good eyes could find?"

"I swear dawn would give me no better sign. The moon is up, Chief. I could not miss their tracks."

Tengis nodded. "Help secure the camp. There are many hours before dawn." He turned to Phayaden. "Go rest now, you have been wounded and you must ride soon."

She nodded, as her own family came to the gher.

She looked at Engidu, as they crowded around them. "There is more to this day than just a fight."

He nodded.

"To you," she asked, "Jekente, and now the path laid down for us?"

"It is," Engidu said with a shrug.

"And what would you have me do?"

"Listen to what I tell you, next time. I told you not to move, but you left Dhuma's gher and came here. Was it worth it?"

"What?"

"What you came to find. Would it have mattered as much to anyone else?"

She looked up into his eyes, wishing she had never found him and invited him into the hospitality of her family's ghers. His eyes were ancient, and he looked very tired, but the *vhagas* and even the *u'wuhshu* of him filled the room, no longer red, no longer angry, but solid and real. She felt tears coming down her cheeks. "No. It wouldn't. It means something only to me."

One hand touched her shoulder. "*Bogeh*," he said. "Nothing is ever so silent."

It felt like an apology.

Mab Morris

III

"You will want these things," said Phayaden's mother. Edhen picked up the needles and thread and dye sticks Phayaden had dumped earlier, and reached for the bag they had once been in.

Phayaden clutched the bag that now only had the broken *Khémèresh*. She knew her sister had envied the needles and other implements. "Nahven has wanted them. Give them to her."

The small woman looked up at Phayaden. "She already has needles," Edhen said. Her shoulders were hunched from sewing, milking horses, and felting. She lifted the dye stick and needles in two hands towards her daughter, trying again.

Phayaden shook her head, shoving the small pile over to her mother. "No, all of it."

Phayaden did not want these things. The torn pages inside her embroidered bag were more important—though useless. There was something else she needed, more useful. She stared through the broken wall, to the darkness outside. She could see stars glimmer, but it did not give her peace. She shivered, and not just from the cold coming from the outside. She understood what she did want. None of the objects she had treasured before.

"Even the book?" her mother asked.

"The book?" Phayaden asked startled.

Edhen lifted the copy of Phayaden's *Khémèresh*.

"Oh," Phayaden said, "Yes. Sure. She has wanted to read it."

"But Phaya! It is your *Khémèresh*. You are our *Bogeh*!" She began to stand up, to be heard by the others. The others packing their possessions in the room were beginning to look at them.

Phayaden shook her head, and gave her a smile

that felt weak in her own face. "It is well, Mother. Nahven should be reading this one soon."

"You're sure?" Edhen asked. "Oh! I did not realize. Should you not tell her?"

Phayaden realized in her distraction that she'd led her mother to believe that giving her sister the book might mean more than it did, that Nahven might be able to study as a *Bogeh*. "It will not matter if she knows, only time will tell, but still—do not tell her," she said awkwardly, and stood to walk through the broken wall. "She must still learn to read the words."

Clutching the bag she looked around. She did not know if she should speak to Engidu about what she wanted, or Tengis. Taking deep breaths of cold night air, she trembled and waited. She saw Tengis first, coming back from the hills on a horse with a saddle not decorated for his own men. He conferred with his commander Ghobi, noticed her and nodded.

She waited. He finished, and slid off the horse.

Ghobi lead it with others they had gathered from their fallen enemies, those that had not been ridden away or run off. He came to her.

"Are you well?"

"I would like a knife," she said.

"What?" He was shocked. "But you are *Bogeh*."

She closed her eyes, clutched the book in its bag. Opening her eyes, she looked up at him. "I do not expect you to understand. A knife, and the learning to use it."

"Why?"

"For a symbol of what I am."

"I do not understand."

"I do not expect you do. I cannot explain it," she admitted only because she was not quite sure what she really wanted. "But please may I have a knife?"

"It is not because you were wounded, attacked?" He took one of her arms, and through the cut cloth, felt the bandage there. "My brother hurt you. I do not know what demon led him to hurt both a friend and a *Bogeh*, but this wound, here… could have killed you," he said pointing to her wrist.

She nodded. "I know this," she said tapping her healer's bag on her left hip. "And it is not that…it is partly that, but not for the reasons you imagine. I am on the wrong path, and must get to the right one."

"And a knife will help you do it?"

"Yes," she said, then shook her head. "No, not to use it." She stomped her foot on the hard ground. "Would it help if I said it is something of the *vhagas*? There is a mystery there I must learn. It has something to do with knives."

"If you brave the *vhagas* again, little one, I would give you ten such knives."

"One will do."

"Are you certain you wish this, Phayaden?" Tengis asked, still worried.

She shrugged. "I am not very brave, but yes."

"That is sufficient for me. But if you wear it

openly, everyone will know how mad you have become."

She snorted. "My family already guesses, but how far… only The One in *The Khémèresh* would know."

"And He would be to blame."

"Or She," she said.

His eyes glinted with humor. "Come. But to teach you…. When? I do not know."

"You will find time," said Engidu rising up from the shadows of the gher's broken walls.

"You have been there all this time?" asked Tengis.

"All what time? I have been here forever."

"And you do not think what she does is wrong?" Tengis asked.

"I am *Bogeh* enough to know that all three of us are on the wrong path."

"You…" began Phayaden.

"Wrong path?" Tengis cried. "I have been made Chief of the Rheshi!"

"Oh. You're not doing anything wrong. Neither am I. I have been doing what I have been told to do, created to do. I, perhaps, missed a vital point. As have you. As have both of you, even now."

Phayaden turned to look at the hills and the night sky, shaking her head.

"You think I'm wrong?" Engidu asked her.

She turned back to look at him. She was trembling and clenched her fists to hide it. "It has been far too strange a day and night. Can I not be done?" Phayaden exclaimed.

"It was strange long before you met me. I can't change the things you have seen and done today," Engidu said gently. His blue eyes were kind, but looked as if they had seen more than a lifetime of history.

"She has been cut and beaten, is that not enough?" Tengis demanded.

"The Tashihyel is rotten with more holes than those dug by ground rats. It should not take you more than one cut woman to know that—and a *Bogeh*! A small one, very frightened, hurt by a man that has been named a friend. As 'mad' as she is, even she knows how woven this day has been by that which is *vhagas*. As do you!"

Tengis shook his head, stepped back. "No. It is foolish."

"Was it not enough that your brother came to attack your ghers? Do you think he did not notice your banners, once they were up? Had not seen them because it was night?"

Tengis also turned away, and was silent. Dawn lit the edge of the hills before he spoke. "It is my sorrow that he did this, my shame that he nearly destroyed this *Bogeh* woman. Would you have me do more?"

Engidu shrugged his shoulders. "I can only guide you in this test of your vision and resolve my friend."

The Red Khémèresh

"Are you my friend?"

"More than any. What is more, I do not even want position in your government, your ghers, or your people. I am only here till this crisis finally moves towards its conclusion. The rest is up to you."

"An odd choice?" said Phayaden. "You would not stay longer?"

"I have met such battles before. If Tengis wins, he will not need me." Engidu shook his head. "I am content. I do not need to stay. I have done what I could, and hope one day to soon be on my own path. My true path."

"So, even *Bogeh* struggle to find their way?" Phayaden asked.

"As The One might wish," he said and strode away.

They watched him walk away.

"One strange man, Phaya, that you found on the steppes."

63

She nodded. "Almost more odd than I. Perhaps I like him more because of it."

"Trust him more because of it?"

"Is it trust? I think with him it does not matter."

"Well, come then. For your knife."

"You do not like that Jekente used his knife on me."

"Bows and arrows, wrestling, eagles. Tools of war. In battle I can understand Swords, spears and knives. But what Jekente did to you was not even like a hunt, where one pits the skill of hunter against the nature of the prey. There is no bravery or mercy in cutting an unarmed woman."

She knew honor and respect, even in battle, even against an enemy was important to him. She had a brief vision that one day he would have a general from an enemy become a trusted counselor. "I cannot think when last your arrows went off your chosen mark. Is that mercy to pit such accuracy against your prey?" She teased him.

He shrugged. "Even when standing in my saddle, with my horse at his best speed?"

"Yes."

"Well, maybe it's not fair at that," he said with a grin, "but I cannot even think to when last I saw you with any weapon in your hand, even a hunting bow since you became a *Bogeh*."

"It was wrong then."

"You are still *Bogeh*, aren't you? But..." he stopped, looked down at her, "Engidu is right. This has been a strange day." He paused and said softly, "But it *has* been odd for a long while, has it not?"

She nodded. "We've both seen it in different ways."

In his gher he found her a knife, helped her strap it to her right leg, where it could hide under her pale coat. "Well, at least fewer people will comment on it here," he said.

She agreed. "I do not think I wish this to be quite out in the open as to carry it in my hand all day."

"Besides, how would you ride?"

"Indeed."

He sat her down outside his gher, on her saddle. "Sit. You are the most wounded person in this camp, and the only *Bogeh* besides, except for maybe Engidu, but who would believe him if he spoke of such things? He has no braids. You rest till we ride."

IV

Phayaden found it boring to watch everyone work. Tengis's gher was down to wood when her mother Edhen found her. She was carrying a thin pancake stuffed with meat.

"Engidu's eagle caught this. He said to cook you some meat before we left. You lost a lot of blood, daughter. You must be well enough to ride when we go."

Phayaden took the food. "Thank you, *aneyh*," she said as her mother patted her hair and also put Phayaden's hat beside her.

Phayaden stared at the pancake stuffed with cooked fowl. At first she did not want it, but she knew that it would help quiet her mind, lessen the sense of the *vhagas* that still lingered in the camp. Both were too raucous. She ate, and found that she was drowsy again.

She had been up most of the night. Hugging her knees, she pillowed her head in her arms and slept.

Engidu woke her. Her brother Paybas stood there with her horse. Paybas had put the saddle on the mare's back, while Engidu steadied her.

"We must now deal with the dead," said Engidu. "Three of our enemies lay fallen." He helped her into her saddle.

Phayaden nodded. "So many…" she whispered. "I have mourned only three people in this harsh land. My family is small. Now three more in one night? You will help?"

"How I can. As we are leaving, and as they were enemies… we leave them where they have fallen."

"Who arranged the bodies?"

"I did."

"You? But were no men of Tengis's camp kin to these men. His brother…"

"They were enemies, Phayaden. Come, the camp

must go soon. They are already leaving."

"Then who is that?"

"Tengis. He will not come near, but will guard us as we do our job."

Phayaden realized that Engidu had not truly left them where they had fallen, but near enough. He had taken the bodies further into the wilderness, away from the small lake and stream, away from the water. However, he had not given them the courtesies of a family member. He put them near each other, but not too close. Phayaden prayed over each man, not bothering to get out of her saddle. Engidu had left them naked and yet clothed their faces in white cloth.

"Is it enough, do you think? Will Jekente come back for his men?" She asked him.

"He will not, but we have done what we could. It is more than they deserve, but Tengis and your family could not have the onus of leaving them, especially not leaving them near a good campsite."

She hoped it was sufficient. If the bodies were not cursed, the wilderness would have them: their bodies and souls transformed by time, weather, insects, and animals. She was not happy, but they had done what they could. It was more than other families might do. Neither Tengis nor her family would do less.

She nodded and they rode to meet Tengis. Together, they rode to meet the camp. When they met with the Dhuma's household and Tengis's men, Phayaden moved to ride beside her uncle.

"There you are, my sister's daughter. We have agreed to ride to Gheber Rocks for now, where there will be a larger encampment of Tengis's men, and possibly a contingent from his father, Toberackhs. Surely the man must consult his father, before meting justice out to a man who would attack both brother and a *Bogeh*."

She nodded.

"You are silent."

Phayaden turned to him. He was standing, and

gently swaying with his horse's bouncing rhythm. His arms were crossed, though one hand still held the reins. He was nearly as sturdy as Tengis, but somehow softer. His dark eyes were framed by lines of laughter, and his beard ready to echo smiles rather than grim determination. The lines of his shoulders, however, seemed to sag more than they had.

"I did not mean to ignore you, uncle. Are you comfortable traveling with all these men?"

"How could I do otherwise, when more warring clans come and attempt to claim our pasturage, and one such as Jekente would attack a young woman who had been his friend, and for no reason. Men might think you mad, but what to say of a man who would do this? Your braids make you no longer safe? How could this be and still afford us protection?"

"I am sorry."

"For what?"

"That I could not be a better *Bogeh* for you."

71

"Perhaps there will come a time when a small family can travel the Tashihyel alone, without fear of another clan or family attacking. That day has long been gone. You afforded me and your mother a few years of freedom."

"They brought me peace as well, uncle."

"Then they were worth still more."

They rode in silence a while longer. Phayaden's attention kept wandering to Engidu's eagle, and where he rode alone when his bird flew in the steady wind of the Tashihyel. Horse, man and bird seemed to fly together. His coat, minus one ring, was tied against the wind that carried his bird in gliding arcs, and let his horse's mane and tail seem to dance.

"Are all three tame, or all three wild, do you think?" asked Phayaden.

"And what do you think is tame, my girl?" asked Dhuma. "Our horses must be caught and broken almost each time we ride. Our dogs tied when any stranger comes...." He stopped speaking, when he caught her eye. "But I understand. The *Bogeh* in you comes from this side of the family. His clothes are strange, his saddle a little odd, and his horse's reins barely in use. The eagle is never hooded, and the man has no glove but lets the beast sit upon his arm, as if her claws could not break his wrist with a thought."

"Much less pierce the cloth and make him bleed," she said.

"But all these things, his clothes, his saddle, are not arts to..." he paused, shook his head. "I am pretending, Phaya, that I have anything to say. I can say this: He is as natural and as cruel as his bird. Wild? Tame? They are just words, like those in a book. He may play your *ushadaz* very well, but they are just the same as the words on paper."

"Words on paper tell us things, uncle."

"*Aven*, of course, but they only rise from the meaning and hide it too. If the *ihyel* were simple,

73

without *vhagas*, or… well… without too many men, and cultures and people, then that man there would have no need for saddles, or clothes, or… words. Do you not think this, daughter of my sister?"

She watched the three a moment longer. "But he embraces the words as well. They are his work as well as his playground. I think he is lost in the *ihyel*, somehow."

Phayaden felt the eyes of her uncle on her a long while. When she looked at him, his eyes were thoughtful. "What?" she asked him.

"You are speaking more like a *Bogeh* than you have in a long while."

Her horse felt her sudden fear and began to jump.

"Would you have me glad to see you run from that which you were born to do?" he asked her.

For a moment she could see on his face that he had dared to speak of things long unspoken. She had seen that look upon his face, once, when the question of life and death were held in the fragile balance of one small breath when a foaling horse was about to die, with the foal as well. This time it was her life. He did not know if she was of this world, the *ihyel* or the *vhagas*.

She could not speak, and kicked her horse away from him, heading past where Engidu rode his horse and raced his eagle.

Mab Morris

V

Both Tengis and Engidu caught up with her, and forced Phayaden's horse to slow down as a team.

Tengis demanded, "Why did you ride off like that?"

She shook her head, and did not look at him. He moved his horse to see her face. She could not turn or she would have to look at Engidu.

"You have been crying. Why?"

"My uncle has said I sounded like a *Bogeh*. He was glad."

"I do not understand!" Tengis threw up his hands. "I took you back to him, thinking this would help you be happy. I never understood. What is wrong? You must tell me!"

"I will lead your horse, you talk," said Engidu.

77

He threw his eagle into the air, which pierced the silence with a cry before it disappeared into the horizon.

"I do not want to be like them," Phayaden said.

"Like whom?" Tengis asked, reaching over and grasping her arm.

"The *Bogeh*. I cannot. What... it is... It's all words. There was a time when I would have burned every *Khémèresh* I could find, but it's not wrong. Nor are the *Bogeh* when they read it, or when they rise along the *bhaganhev* and through the smoke hole into the *vhagas*. They are not wrong when they tell those people living in the *ihyel* what is in the *vhagas*, or even the book. But... they are bound. They are bound to the words as they were taught. They become tied either to the words of the book living without spirit in the ihyel, or live only in the *vhagas* and cannot relate to those living here. I cannot do either. I never have. I cannot live in one place or the other, nor live in both."

Tengis had to think for a moment. His near black

78

eyes searched her face, and studied her. The tension in his arms as he held her arm relaxed. He caressed her shoulder and put his hand back on his reins. "You could always see or sense more than everyone."

"Or feel it? No, I do not know that I did; it was always too confused. Too large? But they see the world only as these things… only through the veil of the *vhagas*, or bound to the words of *The Khémèresh*? They cannot see… But I have seen… and I do not know the words, or the meaning. I could not be enough part of both to tell…."

She stopped speaking, realizing some truth of what she said and unable to finish. How could she explain that the *ihyel* and *vhagas* were not always separate for her? That she needed no *bhaganhev* to see the one for the other. That the constant need to be in one or the other as *Bogeh* was exhausting. But, here, now… there was something else. It made her want to run again, to kick her poor horse into its wild, bouncing trot, ride like only those of the Tashihyel could do, swaying in her saddle, without thought, without needing to think of either body or thoughts.

"Enough!" said Engidu. "You have cried. We have heard. You have not yet, even now, brought yourself onto the right path. You keep running from it."

She looked up at him in surprise, and saw that Tengis had been surprised as well.

"But you are close."

"Close," she said, confused.

He shrugged. "You would bleed instead of embrace. But how can you do else when you cannot yet see what you could accept?"

"That cannot make any sense," said Tengis. "Even to a *Bogeh*!"

"It doesn't have to. Now come, you've told your men we will catch up. Perhaps now we can stop and teach Phayaden how to use her knife?"

"And why would we do that right now?" Tengis

asked, angry.

"Because it the opportunity is here, why not take it? Half an hour will suffice, and her horse could rest."

"It is bred for endurance."

"But she has ridden it hard."

"Fine. I'd rather return to the caravan, but I did promise her."

So they slowed their horses, and Engidu took care of them while Tengis showed her how to hold and cut the air to defend herself. Together the three of them went through a very simple form.

"Tonight, in the dark, we can use sticks so that you will see how to connect with an opponent, even if the opponent is an idea," he said when they were finished, and the horses somewhat rested. "Has this helped you any?"

She nodded. "I do not know why. It is perhaps the action of the body, for a purpose other than riding a horse, eating or walking that I need."

"If you were a man, I'd recommend wrestling," Tengis said. "But perhaps we should get you a bow as well?"

"A little too conspicuous," said Engidu, "when she needs to embrace her opposition with a bit more intimacy than the distance of a bow shot. Which is what this knife can teach her. Would that we could be able to attack all our challenges from afar!"

Tengis nodded. "No man can, nor should."

Engidu stopped. He studied the chief of the Rheshi for a moment. Phayaden could read pain and sympathy written in the tightened lines of his face. "You will wish you could," Engidu said softly.

Tengis shrugged. "And yet, Engidu, there is much I can do with my bow, my riders, and my mind."

Engidu leapt to his horse, laughing. "That we shall see!" His horse trotted a few steps away and he turned. "Are you coming? We do not wish to ride these horses too hard before we meet your people."

VI

They were vigilant during the night, yet found trails of riders around their camp when it came light. For two nights, it was like this. On the third, Engidu watched with Tengis, and his eagle flew in the night. It came back with an arrow, its fletching like Jekente's. A howler, as well.

In the morning, as they moved on, Phayaden examined the arrow, riding beside Tengis and Engidu.

"He is pacing us," she said. "I do not understand this arrow, though. A howler you call it?"

"There are many ways to win a battle," Tengis said. "I taught him this. Discourage your enemy first. Arrows of fire, or arrows that howl and scream like demons when they fly to their target," Tengis said.

"Your men know this."

"Dhuma's family does not," murmured Engidu.

"I do now. I will go tell them," Phayaden said.

Tengis shook his head. "It would not matter. This is a device of men, a thing. What Dhuma and your mother and your family fear is not this arrow, or those like it. Nor the horses that he rides. They fear what he has done to you, and what he may do again, that they cannot risk leaving me, nor ever be free of men like me again."

Phayaden looked at Engidu. "You knew this would happen, and you kept him to his word. We burden him."

Engidu shook his head. "No, that is not true."

Phayaden could almost hear him say that she should have said Tengis and his men burdened her family as much as he helped keep them safe.

He added, "And there are more reasons for him to stay by your side than keeping your family safe, or keeping them from fear."

"To give me a knife, perhaps?"

He laughed, "No, not that either. Or perhaps that as well."

"Come," said Tengis, "we must be off. I'm supposed to lead my men, not follow them."

"Is there nothing we can do for my family, to keep them brave?"

"There is an *ihyelouhbu* up ahead," Engidu said. "If we head a bit towards the west, towards the mountains, not by much, we will find it. There... perhaps much will happen. You will lead us there, Tengis?"

"If you guide me."

"That is my duty to you, my friend."

Phayaden laughed, "Yes, Tengis, for now, wherever Engidu guides you, he and I will follow."

Tengis laughed as well, and rode to the front to shift the direction of the caravan towards the mounded shrine of the *ihyelouhbu*.

Mab Morris

VII

They made it to the *ihyelouhbu* in a few hours. They took the time to let each member walk around the mound of stones, say a prayer, leave an object, and then keep on their journey to a new place to camp. Only Tengis, Engidu and Phayaden waited till the end, watching over the offerings and people.

Perhaps it was in having had so many *Bogeh* experiences the past few days, but Phayaden could feel the wishes rising from that which people left there. She did not hide from it. She watched Engidu, who leaned back against the high cantle of his saddle, arms crossed over his chest. His whole body was relaxed and loose. His head had fallen back, as if he were asleep. His face, however, even his fingers, was not still. He laughed silently, once, while one of Tengis' men walked solemnly around the shrine and left his object.

"Have you no grace? This is a sacred thing!" whispered Tengis, who had been silent all this time.

"And if you forget that you are human, even during moments with divinity, then you become profane. Would you have someone be guilty of merely being man?"

"And you claim this for yourself?"

"Not at all. You made more noise than I have. I forgive you, however, for we are still not loud enough to disturb those below."

"You laughed."

"But not out loud. The matter was private. I was as quiet as the man below."

"Both of you need to be silent," Phayaden interjected. "Leave him be, Tengis."

Tengis went back to his silence. Phayaden noticed that he scanned the horizon and the land around them as intently as Engidu seemed to be contemplating the sky. He was waiting for something to happen.

When all the people of the procession had their turn, they made their way down to say their own prayers.

She watched Tengis leave an arrow head, and then in her turn she left a bead from one of her braids. Engidu left nothing. She watched as he walked around the sacred mound. He said nothing; he seemed to listen instead.

Then they got on their horses and followed after the rest of the procession.

"Nothing happened," said Tengis.

"What do you mean?" asked Phayaden.

"At the *ihyelouhbu.* Nothing happened there."

"Who said nothing happened there?" Engidu said, "You did not see it, Tengis, but much happened all the same. You saw it, did you not Phayaden?"

She nodded. "People prayed and felt better. Can you not hear Dhuma laughing? I have not heard him laugh in days," she said lightly, for the surprise was in realizing that Tengis had come to expect Engidu to predict the future. Looking intently at his face, she did not discover that Tengis was aware of it, or that it was a dependence of great note. She allowed herself to fall back a bit, to question why this both pleased and discouraged her.

"And that is all we expected?" Tengis asked.

"And was that not enough?" said Engidu. "You did not see anything but what was on the surface."

"Do the gods really listen?" Tengis asked.

Engidu laughed. "Of this I am certain. But you would not need to question if you trusted this, you would not doubt what you know."

"Then this is good," said Tengis, and kicked his horse to gallop to the head of the procession.

Engidu and Phayaden rode in silence a while longer, then she said, "It is difficult for a *Bogeh* to give their own prayers at an *ihyelouhbu,* is it not?"

"And why do you ask me this? Did you not

pray?"

"I did. I do not think you did."

He gripped the reins. She saw his knuckles grow white. "Why is it that you would see most things, and you refuse to see this," he muttered. She was not sure she heard him, but then he spoke again. "Long ago I loved a woman. I left her. It was good that she remained where she was and I wander away from her garden and the Tree she tended. There was work I was called to do, appointed to me and given to no other, just as she was created to steward this Tree. When I left, I did not know it would be nearly impossible to return to her. What can I pray that I have not already prayed? It is not even as if I do not know how The One understands... It has just been too long."

"How long?"

"Almost my whole lifetime."

"And yet, if she has stayed in one place... how can you not find her?"

His laugh was bitter. "My dear girl, I am in the business you should be in, of all *Bogeh*, if they do their work well. I help great men return to their true paths. In helping people stumbling from their center, it seems I have stumbled away from my own, and there is no one to guide me back."

"I would…" she began, and then knew. She felt the blood drain from her face.

He turned and she saw his eyes. They were even more ancient than before.

"Do not fear, Phaya. I could not expect even one such as you to help me." He paused. "You are not offended?"

She shook her head.

"But you are afraid."

She nodded.

"I cannot think why, when you've had cause to be afraid of far more than I."

"But…"

"What?"

"You are…"

"Think of me as a *Bogeh*, who is just a lot older than you."

She laughed. "Uncle said you were natural, like your eagle, or horse. Like the wind or this land, perhaps? I told him that you played in words, lost in the *ihyel*, though I did not say you were of the *vhagas*."

"Dhuma is a wise man."

"He is great too, you know. You are not here for him, but Tengis?"

"If Dhuma is great as an uncle to Phayaden, and the leader of his family, that is sufficient for him. He is these things, and not contained by these things. There is no limit to his greatness. It is merely a rather quiet greatness."

"And Tengis will be… louder?"

"Oh, indeed, and just as great if I can help him confront the challenge he faces."

"Jekente."

He gave her a wry look. "You see me... and still do not see more than that!"

She thought back to when Jekente had attacked her.

"There was something in his eyes. And... I found myself... floating... I saw a demon face. But it was like a maze. No... a labyrinth, though it was not a simple pattern, it followed only one line. It was his face."

The memory of it returned to her and she dwelt in it, listening to what it had been, what it was. Darkness filled her chest. She could not breathe, and her heart raced as the scream of the vision rose up to her eyes like a physical blow. She felt her body, though standing in her stirrups, move her left foot, and then start to launch herself out of the saddle. She landed on the ground, running towards the east, turning away from the mountains in the southwest. Her ears were roaring with the shriek of this dark creature. Turning back, to see how far she'd gone, Phayaden could still see its dark green edges of the woods in the distance, but could clearly smell the pine, and see the shadows of the forest floor under her hands.

She heard hooves over her. She sensed a deep red shadow and the thundering as hooves stomped upon the ground around her, defeating the dark shadows and demon yell. Silence came, and the vision faded. She could breathe and hear as Engidu and Tengis each grabbed her arm to lift her up. She was further away from the procession than she'd expected.

Engidu relaxed first. "It is gone?"

She nodded.

"What direction?" Engidu asked.

She pointed to the mountains. "He is that way."

"Who is?" Tengis asked.

Phayaden looked at Engidu, at a loss. She could not bring the demon into the same world where Jekente lived and had been her friend—even though her wounds still itched in healing. She could not willingly bring those two together by her own words. She began to shake and cry.

"She is in shock," said Engidu. "From a vision."

"Come, then." Tengis helped her onto his horse, and much to Phayaden's surprise, walked.

Shaking her head, tears began to spill over onto her cheeks. "Stop!" she cried. "I would rather walk, my lord," she said.

He stopped looking up at her in surprise. "What did you call me?"

She was surprised as well. "You are a chief. It disturbs me greatly that you walk. I have never seen a man walk this far, nor yet a chief. I cannot have you lead me." Her hands trembled on the high saddlebow.

"You have been injured, you have had a *Bogeh* vision just riding a horse, you are pale, and weak, and you expect to walk while I ride?"

"Please."

VIII

When they stopped to camp that night, it seemed as if Tengis had truly taken over Dhuma's family. Even before the ghers could be unloaded, Phayaden could see an argument between Dhuma and Tengis was quickly becoming heated. Much to Phayaden's surprise, Dhuma's wife Khitana and her mother were also part of the discussion. Three of them sat on their horses to one side, and spoke to Khitana who was still seated in her camel cart, which held their gher. Phayaden was not close enough to hear all of the argument, but came closer as it was odd that they had not thought to consult her; she began to hear words rising with high emotion.

"We have known each other for years!" Tengis said.

"We have protected our own for that long, and

longer as well!" Dhuma said. "And we do not have the time to observe all the formalities!"

Phayaden heard Khitana say something, but not exactly what; Edhen nodded in agreement.

"Circumstances!" bellowed Dhuma. "And why should she agree?"

There was silence, and they all looked to Phayaden. She moved her horse over to them. "What is it that you discuss?" she asked.

"Tengis wishes to marry you," Edhen said.

Phayaden said nothing, merely looked over at Tengis with a raised eyebrow.

"He wishes to blend our families, distribute his men through our ghers and our family through his," said Dhuma.

"It would not be appropriate to do so without a marriage," Khitana said.

"He wishes to do this tonight."

"Ah!" Phayaden said, understanding the

problem. Her people preferred a long courtship, and a ceremony that lasted three days. "It is an agreement, only, that is celebrated. It is not a *Bogeh* ritual; there is nothing *shuru* about it, magical or…" She stopped and looked at Tengis. "But perhaps he ought to have spoken to me about it first."

"What do you suggest?" asked Edhen.

"Set up camp. He and I will speak with one another. If we come to an agreement, perhaps you, Khitana and Dhuma will think of a way to honor the celebration under the circumstances? We are still under threat of a mutual enemy," she said.

She turned her horse, and went to one of the herders and took his small *bhaganhev*. The pole and loop was normally used for catching horses for riding, but Tengis understood her, as did everyone at the camp. They would go into the hills, place it in the ground and it would serve as a signal for privacy, reaching up like the *bhaganhev* in a gher. She handed this to him, and they rode off.

When he'd put the pole into the ground, he turned to her. "Forgive me."

"Why?" she asked as she hobbled the horses.

"For not asking you before this."

"You were being ruled by much emotion," she said, knowing she had frustrated him earlier. "Now, what is the benefit my family can bring to you, or I bring to your household?"

"You are *Bogeh*, is that not gift enough?"

She sat down and looked up at him, waiting patiently, as dusk slowly deepened. Her silence began to be uncomfortable. "I do not know what to tell you," she said finally. "I have seen... much the past few days, weeks perhaps. The vision is too large for me to understand all of it. I will admit that I am frightened of it. I do not wish to see what I have seen for I do not understand it."

"Does any of this have to do with my brother?"

"Yes, and that is a temporary problem. You will not carry it through your lifetime, or mine. When it is over, you will have no need to protect me from him."

"How do you know?"

She gave him a wry look. "I am *Bogeh*."

"Something you ran from years ago, I might add."

Phayaden nodded. "So you are saying perhaps my value is better as a wife?"

He finally sat down beside her.

"The Tashihyel, it is not good," he said.

"Why do *you* say that? Land is land. Our people strong."

"But divided amongst themselves. There is something wrong here, Phaya."

She thought of the broken book in her saddlebag. "I am surprised you know it."

"Then you agree?"

She nodded. "I have believed it. Something…

Bogeh helped me know it. I did not think that anyone would believe me." She thought to herself, *Engidu would*, but that hardly mattered.

"I cannot do what I wish with my brother as my enemy," Tengis said. "It cannot happen. But if I could unify as many families and clans together… then I might strengthen the Tashihyel and we could defeat our enemies."

"Then you should marry someone stronger, with a larger herd of her own and more family."

"But who else would share my vision?"

"Would you want her to?"

"You said the other day my father believed no man was strong if he did not accept the council of his women."

"And you think me wise enough for that?" she asked, but realized she was seeing more than just his words. The *vhagas* that echoed past the small *bhaganhev*, past the horses, beyond them seemed focused on their little spot. His future seemed to vibrate to the horizon. She could see what Engidu had said about path. This conversation, somehow, would help guide him to his true path, even while she struggled with her own.

"Who else would be mad enough to see what I propose? It is a large vision, and I have not, yet, all the support of the other chiefs. And what other *Bogeh* would look past their book to support me?"

"Vision beyond *The Khémèresh*, then, isn't it."

He nodded. "I need someone who does not think with the patterns our people have made, this life, this culture. They are set in their ways."

"It has made us strong and our horses hardy."

"It is past time for us to be united."

"No, or you would be dead. What if my… madness detracts from your chances?" she asked, though she did not think that it would. But her *Bogeh* vision was not the same as his, which seemed to speed fast in the *ihyel.*

"If I cannot find a way to build upon my own merits and yours, then my vision is doomed to begin with. I am no bad strategist, Phaya. I would not have proposed this if I thought it would doom my chances. I believe I need your wisdom as *Bogeh* or wife. I would like both."

"Then I will say yes to your proposal."

"Thank you. It is not a matter of mere convenience, you understand."

She nodded. Years before she had thought Jekente would have negotiated for her hand. He never had. It had not hurt her, and she had felt no loss. It was possible that his unspoken claim on her had only been to keep Tengis and her apart. Apparently at any cost. For some reason the thing inside Tengis' brother wished to prevent the realization of both their visions. But looking at the man beside her, it was not merely for a hope for the visions of either *Bogeh* or Chief that Phayaden was now glad.

"It is perhaps unfortunate that we will not have much time in the coming days to prove it," she said.

He stood, held out his hand to help her up. They quickly rode back to their camp as dark descended. The camp was set up, with her uncle, aunt, mother and Engidu waiting for them.

"We have agreed," Tengis said.

"Then as we are traveling to meet your father at Gheber Rocks, and we have a common enemy, a shortened celebration will do," said Dhuma. He was not happy, but it would have been ludicrous to reject an offer that could only be called advantageous for his niece, if not his whole family. He nodded at his wife and sister, and they turned away and left.

"While the elder ladies prepare the feast, you and I will confer on the distribution of Phayaden's household. We will assume your gher as a new one, till one can be made for you both. Phaya, get ready in your mother's gher, with the other girls."

She slid off her horse, and Paybas emerged from the crowd waiting outside the gher, to take her horse. "We'll get the horses ready, as well," he said.

Men from both camps began lighting torches and fires, "so you can see," said Paybas. "It is night, not day."

Dressing did not take long, but Edhen came in, taking a moment to talk quietly and privately to her daughter about what to expect, then left Phayaden to her cousins and sisters. They'd not long to prepare, so they put on outer coats from another wedding long ago, embroidered with deep red. Phayaden's cousins and younger sisters gathered what decorations they could for her *Bogeh* braids. They took out the old beads from her braids and let her pick the ones that she wanted. When she finished, she realized all the beads she'd picked were either gold or red. It was not, she realized, for the wedding, but for the Horseman and what had greeted her beyond his shoulder. That she would marry, with colors that echoed the vision… She felt a red hoof stomp the ground, with a sound that vibrated her whole horizon…. An echo of the Words rang as well. The choice was good.

The girls and young women emerged from the gher, and quickly got into their saddles, the little ones being helped by brothers. Paybas stopped Phayaden for a moment. "A few of us, and Tengis's men are going to be riding out with you, to guard, but not too close, you understand? But I and Tika are going to ride with you to announce your arrival."

"Tika first, I assume?" she asked.

"He is little."

She nodded. "A feast, in my mind, would have served just as well."

"That I grant you," he said, "but Dhuma insisted. He is aware of our unequal wealth and position."

"It mattered not to Tengis."

"He is right, though, Phaya. In this way, with so many witnesses, even among his own men, he cannot easily cast you aside."

"I could leave him too, brother."

"*Aven*, but if we keep discussing it, we will be late for your feast."

They got on their horses, rode out a distance. A good guard of men stood still in their saddles a good distance away, bows ready. She could see them quite well enough as the moon rose above the hills.

"A good moon," she said.

Paybas nodded, and sent Tika off. They could hear the shouts of greeting when he arrived. A few moments later, Paybas rode off. Phayaden turned to Nahven. The girls were all a bit nervous, starting at shadows and stray winds.

"We are very alone out here," said Nahven.

"There are men to guard us," Phayaden pointed out.

The Red Khémèresh

"They are far off, and… we are still afraid. Could you have chosen a better time for this?"

They heard the shout of greeting for Paybas.

Phayaden told Nahven, "This wedding serves to protect us even more, even if we are vulnerable out here, for a moment. Come, they await us."

"Our tears, then, will be of relief."

"Then let us ride fast!" said Phayaden with a shout, suddenly happy. In days of fear and strangeness, even with this contracted wedding, it felt good to ride fast with the girls, as if they were free and fearless. The other girls caught her mood.

With laughter, they rode to the camp, faster than they might have otherwise.

Nahven led the way, and rode around the whole camp, letting their horses prance and dance. "Bells!" cried Nahven, and they dug into their pockets and brought out their music bells. Singing and laughing, they chimed their bells, as they rode around Tengis's gher three times. They stopped at the doorway.

"And who would you marry?" asked Nahven.

"That woman there," said Tengis, and went to her to help her out of her saddle.

Standing with him, she took his hands. Paybas and the rest of the camp unsaddled horses and activity swirled around them. "Is it good?" he asked in a low voice.

"Yes."

People from five ghers crowded into Tengis's. It was fortunate that it was the largest one, even over Dhuma's. They feasted on the *toub* Phayaden had found days ago, and meat and even the little ones drank enough *aghika* to get tipsy and make it necessary to milk the mares. Adults drank *walika* when, finally, the roast lamb came in from outside.

"They started as soon as we rode off," Tengis said, "starting the fire as quickly as they could, even before the ghers were up. The coals from your mother's brazier filled its gut."

"What would they have done if we'd not agreed?"

"Your mother and aunt were pretty confident, though Dhuma was not."

"Ah. There will not be much left for the dogs, tonight."

"Just as well, as they must not be sluggish tonight, to help guard."

"I may have had too much *walika*."

He shrugged, "Neither you nor I will be guarding tonight."

Phayaden smiled at him, but was grateful when Engidu began to play her *ushadaz* and sing. Everything seemed so huge, matching in size and strength her vision of the Horseman. He had filled the horizon, but he was now joined by more than Himself. The gher was filled with warriors, and though the Horseman of her vision had been naked, she had known He was a man of war

111

and strength. The firelight, the reflection of red from the girls' clothing and the weapons that leaned against the wall made each man seemed to reflect that Warrior. She looked at Tengis. He seemed touched by the Horseman most of all. And there was Jekente, somewhere out there to the southwest. The demon that possessed him also loomed large.

Tonight, even alone, embracing Tengis, she would somehow be embracing them all. They were as part of Tengis as his hair. Part of his future, or fate. Part of hers.

Engidu finished his song, and the party was somehow over. Everyone filed out and went to their ghers, or on guard duty.

"I will be watching all night," said Engidu to Tengis.

"You need your sleep, man. There are others to guard the night."

"Oh, I will rest as much as needed, but I will

help guard too, against those things men cannot watch for, but I can. Good night, to you both," he said.

Phayaden was glad that Engidu had made a point of saying it. She knew he would be guarding against that which was not man. She watched him step over the threshold. The door closed and Tengis turned to her where she stood in the women's side of the gher.

She felt her fingers trembling, and clutched her hands together. "I have never seen a gher so empty at night before."

"I would guess you haven't."

"Even those who would have been part of my household have left. I did not realize that they…" she stopped. Heat was rising to her face.

"I asked for this. The situation was already different enough for me to ask this. It felt to me as if… events would be complicated enough in the next few weeks to prevent a more usual time for us to know each other better as man and wife."

She nodded.

He stood there for what felt like a long moment. "I believe your women would…" he stopped, shook his head and laughed at himself. "Come, we need not be this formal with each other, now, do we?"

She shook her head. "No."

He reached for her and touched her face, drew closer and kissed her.

It was awkward and strange to undress before a man, and be undressed and help undress that same man. They did not have to be careful. Careful not to see the other side of the gher, careful to protect the privacy of those around them in the open space of a gher, even of married couples. They did not have to be careful not to be of too much notice, either.

The moment they both realized the strange freedom, their eyes met.

However his life had been bound, she did not know. Hers had been bound by the rules of being a

Bogeh, an unmarried daughter, of being mad, having visions and being unable to share them. She still could not, but it didn't matter. He filled her whole horizon, and all those things that had been so very large earlier were of no matter. They were still present. Still of great note. But now they were merely part of the landscape that included his eyes and his body.

His hand touched her breast, and then he leaned in to kiss her mouth.

She reached up to touch his shoulders, and felt the warmth of his skin, let her hands travel, feeling the hard muscles of his arms and back against her palms. He lifted her and carried her to his bed.

None of it was as her mother had led her to expect. A brief thought entered her mind that perhaps Edhen's husband had not been much of a lover, but neither had needed passion to be very happy with each other. As a *Bogeh*, she was educated enough to know that her virginity could not be tested as intact as if she had lived in a land where girls rarely rode horses. It was a matter of trust, and not even a requirement for their contract. None of this mattered to either Tengis or Phayaden at all.

When he entered her, it was only part of all the intimacy that had gone on before, the friendship they had shared for years, burst in a moment full flower. After the orgasm had spent them both, he lay beside her, still caressing her.

"I believe I was wrong."

"About?"

He shook his head. "I am glad we have a lifetime together. I believe I must ensure we have more time without attendants in future."

"Many, many more?"

"Indeed."

She felt his fingers travel the scars Jekente had left, and even the bruises. "Was I too rough?" he asked.

"No. May I ask… you were married before?"

He laughed lightly. "To answer the real question, yes to both."

"Both?"

"I have had lovers besides a wife."

"I never met her."

"I am older than you by a few years, Phaya. I married her when I was younger, before I became a chief. She was my uncle's niece from his wife's family." He was caressing the scars on her arm. "It is interesting to see these, and realize that Jekente helped me rescue her when she'd been kidnapped by my uncle's enemy and mine. She was not hurt by them. She died a year later in childbirth."

Phayaden did not know what to say, and the pause gave room for the concern they had all been facing for days. "Is he angry because he is not chief, and he is your mother's eldest son?"

"Perhaps. He does not see that it is not through my father's name I earned my place as chief, or his father that he did not. The Rheshi may have wished for such an alliance with Toberackhs, but had Jekente the merit he could have gained that title with them. My mother's people are not fools."

He lay back. "I do not wish to talk of him."

"Nor do I." She lifted herself onto an elbow, glad that she did not feel the weight of everything. She caressed him with her fingers. "Tell me what you would like," she said and felt soft skin harden in her hands.

"That is nice," he said.

They did not sleep much that night, but did not feel the loss of it. They woke early, made love again, and then dressed. When they emerged, it was clear that all had not been well in the night.

IX

Phayaden watched Tengis's shoulders stiffen as he stepped over the threshold of their gher.

"What happened? Why was I not informed?" he demanded of the first person he saw.

The sun was not yet up, but there was enough predawn light for the whole camp to see what angered him. She could see it over his broad shoulders as he finished tying up his coat. His banners had been defiled, and a line of arrows embedded into the ground surrounded what could have been the light perimeter of the camp. She knew, however, that Tengis would never have let firelight obscure the night vision of his men.

Ghobi, his commander said, "We did not know. Clouds obscured the moon, and we had no light till now."

Tengis looked over at Engidu. "Can you scout? Can your eagle bring us any evidence of where Jekente is?"

Engidu nodded. He did not look at Phayaden, but she saw he'd stilled an inclination to turn to her. Only one finger trembled against that movement. He knew that she'd known where Jekente was. She had pointed in the direction only the day before. "Of course," he said. "At once." He whistled for his horse.

"You really do not tether him?" Tengis asked.

"No need. He travels with me," Engidu said as he launched himself into the saddle and rode off.

Dhuma rode up to Tengis. "Do we break camp or stay?"

"We stay. Toberackhs cannot help us. I think I must face Jekente, and ask for peace."

"Chief," said Ghobi, "He will have his army with him."

"Not in the forest," said Phayaden.

The Red Khémèresh

"What?"

She shook her head. "Part of a vision. Forgive me, but I think he will go to the forest."

"Whichever direction he is in, wherever he is, I want half the men to stay here, guard Dhuma and his family. We go and see if he can fight in daylight or discuss the matter with his brother."

"He must side with you, Chief. He is one of the Rheshi. He must be made to declare."

"And that is sacred," Tengis admitted, "but would you have the *Bogeh* come with, when he has wounded her?"

Ghobi stiffened. "My chief, just because she is your wife, and even if her own family says she has gone mad, she is still *Bogeh* enough to witness a sacred clan affiliation."

Tengis looked at Phayaden. "Or execution," Tengis said softly.

She nodded, understanding the requirements of

his vision. If he were to create what he wished not even his brother could defy him. "Loyalty must be among the most important virtues of the people in felt houses," was all she said.

He squeezed her hand.

It was boring to wait for Engidu after all that had gone on before. Phayaden knew Engidu had a better idea of where Jekente and his men were because of her vision. He would not be gone long. Only long enough to have done his work as an ordinary man might. They could be leaving as soon as he returned, or stay. Tengis' men prepared for battle.

When Ghobi saw him on the horizon, he alerted Tengis. Within moments, Tengis and his men were in their saddles, riding out to him.

"He is there," Engidu said pointing towards the pine covered mountains pointing in the direction Phayaden shown him the day before. "He does not have but eighteen men with him. They are breaking camp."

"Then we go."

Ghobi turned back to command those that would guard the ghers.

The ride was not hard, or long for they rode with speed. When they found Jekente and his men, it was clear that negotiations were impossible. As one, all Jekente's riders turned and a volley of arrows flew at Tengis and his men. Geared for war, the arrows did not hit them, or hit armor and shields. Much to their surprise, Jekente's men surged forward, spears ready.

Tengis gave a command, and his men raced forward to meet them. Only Engidu and Phayaden held back. When they clashed, Phayaden heard the sounds of weapons and shields and yells. The hooves of the Red Horseman's Horse thundered within the small battle. She could almost see Horse and Rider above them, as solidly as the men who battled below Him.

Curling up from that vision, like an arrow aimed at her, came a shout. Jekente's demon face spiraled towards her, almost obliterating Horse and Rider. One rider broke from the skirmish and sped towards them.

Phayaden and Engidu had little time to prepare. Spear ready, Jekente went straight for Engidu. When the spear did not pierce him, he used it to punch Engidu clean off the saddle.

Jekente turned to Phayaden's horse, dropped his spear, grabbed the reins from her hands, and kicked both hers and his horse into action.

"Humna!" shouted Engidu, "By Gods what are you doing?"

They sped to the pine mountains where demons lived. The sound of the Rider and battle faded. Phayaden knew that Tengis and Engidu would follow, and not too slowly. She felt the uncomfortable weight of the knife on her thigh and was glad yet again.

"Why are you doing this?" she shouted.

Jekente turned to her. Though she could see his face underneath, as if covered in a transparent mask, the face was that of the labyrinthine demon. It spoke, but she understood not a word. And it laughed at her for not understanding, and they rode on, their horses racing as if demons chased them. The whole distance she could not see that anyone had followed.

They entered the woods. Here he slowed, but led her unerringly deeper into the woods. He knew where he was going. He clearly had a plan for which she could not guess at. It was disturbing to realize that Engidu might not know either.

They went past one thicket of trees and came upon a very white gher. What light came through the pine branches, the white felt gleamed like the moon or stars on a clear night. She had never seen anything that bright. Jekente tied the horses up, and held out his hand to help her down.

"No," she said, and tried to kick him away, but he grabbed her leg and pulled her off the horse. She felt as if he were splitting her apart till she hit the ground, landing on her back.

She tried to grab her knife, but he seized her wrists and bound them together. He pulled her upright and dragged her to the gher, though she fought as best she could. He opened the door and pushed her inside, making her trip over the threshold.

Staggering, falling to one knee, tripping over the threshold felt like the worst luck of any in the past days. She looked up at him in horror. "What are you going to do with me?"

Without a word he approached and punched her. The world went black.

X

Though there was sound, it was like water flowing in a river. What she woke to first was the gher's *bhaganhev*. She stared at it, making no sense of the noise she heard, or any other site. The gher's false tree was less carved than any she'd seen. Its simplicity gathered her up the smooth trunk to the branches. As she sat up, she realized the ceiling, and even the floor was decorated in the lines of a labyrinth. The *bhaganhev* was centered inside the innermost turn. Only then did she realize that two men knelt on either side of her. She focused and recognized Tengis first, and then Engidu. Then she heard them speaking.

"...you're awake. Where did he go?" Tengis asked.

"Who? Humna?" she asked.

"No, Jekente."

"Oh…" but she knew where he had gone, somehow. She shook her head. "I don't know."

Engidu slapped her face. He was angry. She looked at Tengis. He was clearly angry as well, though not at her. "He has gone too far, Phaya. Where did he go?"

"He hit me. I did not see."

Engidu stood, looking up at the ceiling, down at the floor. He walked, paced part of the labyrinth's path. "But you know!"

She turned her head. Her shoulders shrank into her body and she realized her arms were not bound. Her jacket was off, knife gone. She was clothed, but Tengis had good reason to be angry, regardless.

"Engidu, she is in shock. The lump on her head is already swelling, whatever else he did to her," Tengis said. She became aware of his hands upon her head and shoulders.

"But she *did* see!" Engidu shouted.

She looked up at him. "Yes, I did," she said softly. "And the Red Rider."

He knelt down beside her again, shaking his head. "You saw the whole and it frightened you."

She nodded. He closed his eyes and sighed. The firelight had stopped flickering. "You know what I am?" he asked.

"That you are not a man. A Guide?"

He nodded. "As is Humna. He is the reason I cannot return to Avensen. He challenges all men against their truest goal. But I have killed him, helped kill him thousands of times," he sagged beside her, very tired. The light of the unmoving fire glowed upon his face. She did not turn to see if Tengis knelt unmoving as well. "Even I cannot get past him. How does one kill him one time more? How do I kill him, when I have done so many times before? Tengis may kill Jekente, killing Humna. Even so, I will face him again, another day, with another man, guiding him to his battle. I do not have a guide past him. Phaya, even if I cannot defeat him for myself, Tengis *must* go face this battle with his brother."

"With Humna."

"With Humna, and for Jekente's loyalty or without it, for that is Tengis' battle. Not yours. This land is broken and needs a leader. The Horseman rides for him. You saw it, everything."

"It is too much. I am frightened. I am *Bogeh*, but who would hear me? Knowing all this means nothing. They will not hear me!"

"Do they need to? Does Tengis need to understand your vision? To be guided by it? He must go to this fight. You are stopping him."

She looked at the frozen world. Sitting with the creature beside her. "I am frightened."

"Yes, and that is your challenge. But are you more than your fear?"

She looked at the godling beside her, the frozen

fire, the echoes of the creatures outside, of the Horseman, of Humna and even the *bhaganhev* which seemed to sound loudly in the small gher.

"Yes," she said though it was terribly difficult to say it.

"Then embrace it."

Ihyel and *vhagas* came upon each other, as light flickered in the gher, and on Tengis's face. "He has gone that way. He is alone, armed, but he will wrestle," she said.

"How do you know?" Tengis asked.

"Do you doubt, or fear?" she asked.

"Come," he said to Engidu. "She will be safe here." He turned to her. "My men are outside."

And then she was alone in the *ihyel*. In the *vhagas* she saw that Tengis and Engidu approached where Humna waited, but she did not know how Tengis fought Jekente. She did not see any of it. She lay back down, rose up with the *bhaganhev* and out of the smoke hole. The Rider stood there, again acknowledging her before he rode off. Still rising through the smoke hole of Humna's gher, through the center of his labyrinth, she embraced all she had seen, even the memory of the brilliancy the Rider had guarded her from.

She walked the path of the labyrinth that was in both worlds of the whole world. She walked to the center, deep into the *vhagas*. To her surprise, she approached a fruit tree. A woman stood up from the shadows under its branches. Her face was young, but her black hair, long, thick, and luxurious with curls glistened with grey.

"I am Avensen. How goes it with Engidu, the Wanderer?"

"He sorrows for you, I think. Are you the love he spoke of? Steward of a tree?"

The woman smiled. "I am. And is Humna well?"

Phayaden smiled. "He is guarding, and challenging, and apparently dying."

The Red Khémèresh

"Then he is also well, but words are too much... and too little for these matters. Shall I show you this Tree?"

Phayaden accepted. Though there were words that came from Avensen's mouth, like song, like history, even parts of *The Khémèresh*, it was not as words that Phayaden heard them. She could hear the Tree, smell it, taste it even, and see into its veins, the rings of it, as well as deep into the ground where its roots moved the earth over time.

She looked as the story of its being moved up the trunk and into the branches, and finally to the fruit. The Tree, part of this conversation with both women, bent a branch down to display the fruit.

Phayaden reached up to touch it. Both Tree and Avensen seemed to hold their breath as her fingers touched the smooth red fruit. She then touched the branch, and the leaf beside it, and the world seemed to shimmer around them. Phayaden sensed the lingering echo that this moment had gone wrong before, at another time, with another woman. She could feel the tree shiver in the memory of the fruit taken too soon, before the woman had understood the whole of its story. Phayaden nodded and started to withdraw her hand, not needing more than she had. In this moment the leaves seemed to clap and dance in the breeze. With a soft snap, the fruit fell. Phayaden caught it with a gasp.

"Oh!" She exclaimed, frightened, still hearing the older story still echoing from the past.

"It is right, my dear," Avensen said with a smile, touching Phayaden's arm. "Now go."

She awoke in the gher, fruit still in her hand. She sat up, and blinked at the *ihyel*, the gher, around her. She almost longed to bite into the fruit, but shook her head and did not. Her eyes caught upon her saddlebags. She stood and pulled out the bag with the broken *Khémèresh*, opened it, and put the fruit beside it. She closed the bag and waited.

The Red Khémèresh

She went back to the fire, and sat back beside the *bhaganhev*. "I am not done here," she realized. She could not go back to being in either *vhagas*, like most *Bogeh*, or in the *ihyel*, like Tengis would. In *The Khémèresh*, there was a word for this state of mind, even if few seemed to understand it. *Ihyelvhagas*. Simple enough a word. *Ihyel* and *vhagas* did not need to be divided, for they were never apart even if most men, including *Bogeh*, could only see one or the other, or depend on only one or the other. It was one of the things she understood now.

She thought to the blazing light behind the Rider's right shoulder. She would certainly never see The One again quite the same way, nor hear Words in the same way either. She could not remember what had been said, but that did not matter for it was as large as the horizon and might have been as simple as, "Hello," or rather "I Am." But she could no longer live as if she didn't know. In breathing quietly, she realized she was not apart from it. Nothing was apart from that which had been behind The Rider.

"What of Engidu?" she asked, still in the *ihyelvhagas*. She knew that being content inside both the world and spirit would not last, but remained calm and listened.

She was answered. He had guided her; she had guided him. She had the apple. Engidu could, now, pass through, for something very important had shifted. He did not need to guide heroes. Men would be challenged within themselves, battles more subtle but perhaps far, far more daunting.

"But he does not know this yet," she said, looking up.

A leaf blocked the light from the hole, and tumbled through the air into her hands. It was not pine like all the trees in the forest surrounding the gher. It was a leaf of the Tree. She smiled, and sat, and waited.

When Engidu opened the door, he smelled of

blood. "Tengis is coming. He and two of his men are going to get the body. Then we will go home."

She stood up. "I think you will, as well," she said and handed him the leaf.

Taking the leaf into his hands, he stared at it. He could not take his eyes off it, but after a moment forced himself to look up at her. "You have an apple?"

"I do."

"Do not be too hasty in eating it. But don't worry. It won't rot before you're ready."

"*The Khémèresh* went wrong then, didn't it? And the Tashihyel?"

"When?"

"I thought… I saw another woman take the fruit. She and another man ate of it. But… it wasn't the eating, was it? It was the taking before she was ready."

"Oh, that happened long before either *The Khémèresh* was written, or the people put up the first felt house." He paused, and then put a hand on hers. "Your apple will not mend it, nor heal the Tashihyel."

She sighed. "I had hoped…"

He touched her arm. "But it is a good beginning."

They rode two days to Gheber Rocks to meet Toberackhs. That Jekente had refused to acknowledge Tengis was noted by the great leader, and his *Bogeh*. They left his body out in the wilderness, mourning his life and his refusal to side with his brother. Toberackhs said to his new daughter, when they returned to his gher. "It is a pity, but he did not have great vision."

The Red Khémèresh

Mab Morris

Glossary

The people of the Tashihyel use some Geberesh words, translated here, with added notes on the uses of the terms. I've added pronunciations, but these are merely how I pronounce them. Reader, please feel free to put your own spin on things, as the book is currently in your hands. If I've done my writing well, you'll not need this except as added entertainment value.

Aghika: [Ah-gee-ka] Fermented mares milk.

Aneyh: [Ahn-eh] A term of endearment for a mother.

Bhaganev: [Baa-ga-nev]. It is the center post of a gher in the Tashihyel, representative of the World Tree. It acts as a bridge between the *ihyel* and *vhagas*. The *Bogeh* use it to help them ground as they rise up into the spirit world. The gher, in fact, acts as a microcosm of the world. The walls represent the material world, the bhaganev acts as the world tree, and the smoke that rises past it and out through the smoke hole above it, represent what happens to the *Bogeh*.

Bogeh: [Bow-geh]   A *Bogeh* is a shaman.   They interpret the spirit world to those who live in the *ihyel*. They are highly regarded, and can overrule chiefs.

Falleh: [Fah-leh]   Is a healing herb

Geberesh: [Geh-beh-resh]   A glossopoeia that primarily focuses on words to describe a philosophy of perception.

Ihyel: [Ee-yel]   The land, ostensibly the material world. It is our world, primarily limited to the material.

Ihyelouhbu: [Ee-yell-oo-boo]   It is a spirit place where people pray and leave a toke of their prayer or hope in thanks.   If the Tashihyel were mountainous, it might be in a grotto or cave, and if it had roads, an altar like shrine.   Being flat, it is a very important mound of stones covered with tokes of various people's spiritual journeys.

Ihyelvhagas: [Ee-yell-vaa-gahs]   It is the world

undivided, where material and spiritual are in harmony... well, they always are, but one could say it's when that balance is also known by a human.

Khémèresh: [Kheh-meh-resh] based on the Ghebereshian term khémè that describes the world we perceive—with whatever senses that we have. Khémè includes the "seen" world, as well as the other, depending on an individual's ability to perceive (and interpret what they perceive) and why each individual is valued. It can mean how we perceive, not just what. Khémèresh, thus, is a spiritual book that helps the Bogeh, and others, to understand the mystery of the world, spiritual and physical.

Toub: [Toob] Call it a potato.

U'wuhshu: [Oo-woo-shoo] It is like the sound of wind upon deep snow at night. It is the lingering sense of what could be called magic, the echoes of the other world, the *vhagas*, upon us.

Ushadaz: [Ooo-shah-daz] A three stringed instrument

played with a bow, based on the Morin khuur of Mongolia. The scene was inspired by listening to a piece of traditional music. I could hear the wind on the grasses, see the horses thundering upon a landscape as vast as an ocean.

Vhagas: [Vaa-gahs] The spiritual side of the material world. It can be described as the world behind the trees where the spirit of the trees might talk with angels or other demi-god like creatures. It is the part of the whole world that is generally unseen.

Walika: [Wah-lee-ka] Call it vodka.

About the Author

"Mab" seems like a funny name for a writer whose work is rather unpopulated by fairies. The name is a portmanteau of the writer's first and maiden name. Having written her first book in high school, with rising hopes of being published, perhaps the Shakespearean queen rode in her hazelnut chariot to midwife those dreams—especially as Mab Morris didn't stop with one book, but ended up writing ten in those subsequent years later, and continues to work on more.

No matter how proud Mab might have been of her maiden name, it wasn't exactly euphonious. After marriage gave her a new last name, making the portmanteau seemed like a fun choice—even if it gave rise to the light, romantic images of Henry J. Ford or Lancelot Speeder rendition of fairies. Her ideas were edgier, like an Arthur Rackham, or, even better, like Rein Poortvleit's work, which while he did works on gnomes and fairies, also had incredible work depicting the natural world.

The Andrew Lang *Colored Fairy Tale Books* helped build a foundation for her work, Ford or Speeder art notwithstanding. The Persian story, written from two different sources, "What the Rose did to the Cyprus" in the *Brown Fairy Tale Book*, is just one example. It is a complex story, and defied the simple ideas of what a fairy story might be. What inspired Mab was that Lang did not limit his gathered tales to just European sources, but gathered folk tales of cultures from around the world. Plenty of Magic in those tales, but surprisingly few fairies.

After writing a number of books, it became clear that Mab's own works would never dance with fairy tunes. More often than not, her work echoes with the otherworld. The novella *The Red Khémèresh*, for instance, introduces a created language with words the shaman Phayaden uses to describe reality: *ihyel* as the natural world that we see around us (and is also the name of the world Mab has been building since the 1980s), and *vhagas*, the unseen world—a world fairies might naturally inhabit. In the shamanism depicted in that book, the real world is actually the *ihyelvhagas*—combining the seen and unseen world. The world is one where Nature and demi-gods work and walk beside the people who change and impact their lives as well. One could say that Phayaden changed the lives of demi-gods, just as much as they influenced hers.

Mab Morris' world Ihyel, and other books that go beyond it, are like Lang's books, or Campbell's *Mask of God* series, in that they reflect the vast, fascinating ancient cultures, folktales, and myths around the world. *The Red Khèmèresh* has foundations in Sumerian myth, as well as Mongolian and Siberian Shamanism.

Forthcoming books, like *Fate of the Red Queen*, have influences from Filipino martial arts, ideas of the origins of the Goddess Kali as described by Joseph Campbell's *Mask of God: Oriental Myths*, and many more. Other sources of inspiration rise from Inuit shamanism, Etruscan myth, Ndembu healing ritual, land based Viking culture, and jaunts into the lore of mythological beasts and creatures.

There may be few immediately identifiable fairies in her work, but there's an ever underlying "not just this realm" in almost all her work. It seemed appropriate that she would choose her littlest book to midwife her dreams of being published, introduce her work to the world, and to display a world that is seen… and unseen.

The Red Khémèresh

Mab Morris

43857543R00085

Made in the USA
San Bernardino, CA
30 December 2016